The adventures of Billy & Penny

Suze Orman

illustrated by KT

About the Author

Suze Orman has been called a force in the world of personal finance and a one-woman financial-advice powerhouse by *USA Today*. She is a two-time Emmy Award winner, the most successful fund-raiser in the history of public television, and the author of nine consecutive *New York Times* bestsellers. *TIME* magazine has twice named her one of the most influential people in the world.

Suze has helped millions of people across the globe transform their lives when it comes to money. She is a firm believer that a financial problem can never be solved with money. As she says, "One has to go within to see why they are doing without."

Now with this book, for the first time she turns her wealth wisdom to the world of kids.

The Adventures of Billy and Penny will help instill values in your children that are needed to build a solid financial foundation.

The goal of this book is to teach kids the importance of counting every penny and making every penny count—a lesson adults can learn from as well.

Library of Congress Control Number: 2016957262

Hardcover ISBN: 978-1-4019-5304-1
E-book ISBN: 978-1-4019-5305-8

10 9 8 7 6 5 4 3 2 1
1st edition, January 2017

Printed in the United States of America

HAY HOUSE, INC.
Carlsbad, California • New York City
London • Sydney • Johannesburg
Vancouver • New Delhi

This book was born out of a promise I made to my dear friend
and mentor Louise Hay, founder of Hay House Publishing.

May we always remember that keeping a promise
is worth more than all the money in the world!

The sun was shining and it was a fresh, crisp morning. Billy stretched.
"Ahhhh! Another great day. Can't wait to see how I spend it."

Billy jumped off the table to make his way to the front door.

All of a sudden, Billy tripped and landed flat on his face on the floor.

As he picked himself up and dusted himself off, he saw he had tripped over his old friend Penny.

"Penny, what are you doing on the floor?
The floor is no place for money."

"Billy, I've been here on the floor for days. You would think someone would have picked me up by now, but I'm telling you—no one values pennies.

"They walk on me. They never save or spend me. They never even notice me."

"No way, that's impossible. You're a penny—honest to goodness money. Every dollar bill is *made up of 100 pennies!*"

Billy and Penny heard someone coming . . . "Watch, I'll show you,"
said Penny. "Billy, quick, lie down right here next to me and don't move."

"Oh, look. A dollar bill. What's that doing on the floor?"

Mom picked up Billy, not even noticing Penny, and placed Billy back into her wallet.

Once the coast was clear, Billy popped his head out of Mom's wallet and saw Penny still lying on the floor. "Penny, Penny, are you okay?"

"Yes, Billy. I'm used to it. I feel like I might as well be invisible.
Everyone has forgotten how much they used to love me.

"You know, Billy, there was a time not so long ago that everyone counted every penny and they made every penny count.

"They would pitch pennies with me.

"They would wear me in their loafers.

"They would save me.

"They would make a wish with me.

"They would pay 'a penny for your thoughts.'"

"That's it, Penny!

"Let's make them start counting pennies again. I have an idea!

"You know how every Thursday night, the family orders the exact same pizza for dinner? They give the delivery person ten one-dollar bills and they always say keep the change."

"Yes, I know that, Billy. But what does that have to do with me?" Penny asked.

"Everything, Penny. We are going to show this family that every penny counts."

Billy leaned over and whispered his plan to Penny.

Billy's idea was to send out
a message to all the nearby
forgotten pennies to meet
up inside the kids' piggy
bank before dinnertime on
Thursday night.

Finally, Thursday night arrived. Billy and Penny were so excited to see if Billy's plan was going to work. They could hear Mom on the phone ordering pizza. "Yep, the usual. See you soon. Bye-bye . . . Kids, get ready for dinner. It's Pizza Night."

As soon as Mom walked away, Billy helped all of the dollar bills to slip out of her wallet and told them to go and hide.

When the doorbell rang, the kids came running.

Everyone loves Pizza Night!

As Mom went to get the door, she grabbed her wallet, only to open it and find it was totally empty. "OH, NO!" she said. "WHERE'S MY MONEY?"

Mom started looking everywhere for money but could not find any.
Then she thought for a second and said, "Kids, hurry and bring me your piggy bank."

The kids ran to go and get their piggy bank. When they picked it up, they said, "I don't remember it being this heavy."

"Here it is, Mom."

"Kids, start shaking out the pennies. We need to count them quickly. The pizza man is waiting."

Finally, the last penny was counted.
"How many pennies do we have, Mom?"

Mom said, "We have exactly 1,000 pennies."

"Mom, how much is 1,000 pennies?"

"Well, there are 100 pennies in a dollar. So 1,000 pennies is $10, and guess what—that's exactly how much we need to pay for the pizza."

Mom gathered all the pennies and put them in two bags, and gave the bags to the pizza man and said, "Keep the change."

The pizza man said, "You bet. You know, my mom always taught me to value pennies— it's good to teach your kids that, too."

As the family gobbled down the pizza, the kids asked, "Mom, what happened to your money? How come you needed the pennies in our piggy bank?"

"Well, kids. When you are not careful with money, you may not really have what you think you have . . . We were all really lucky that you had all those pennies in your piggy bank, or we would not be eating dinner right now."

"Wow, Mom, I never thought about it that way—I guess pennies really do count. From now on, every time I see a penny I am going to pick it up and save it. I have an idea: Let's make a pizza penny jar. Every penny we find, let's put it in that jar and save it until we can buy dinner again."

"Oh, look! There is a penny on the floor over there," the kids said. The boy jumped up and picked up Penny, dusted her off, and put her in the jar.

The next morning, the sun was shining and it was a fresh, crisp morning.
Billy had gotten up early, and to his delight, he looked over and saw Penny
happy in a comfortable jar, nice and clean and shiny.

Billy smiled as he waved at Penny and thought to himself, *Counting every penny and making every penny count really matters, especially if you like pizza.*